MY
GRANDAD
HAS
ALZ–EYE–MURS

BERNADETTE
MUCKIAN

ISBNs:
978-1-80227-951-1 : eBook
978-1-80227-952-8: paperback

A CIP catalogue for this book is available from the National Library.

Dedication

In memory of my dad,

Dr John McCormack

1910 – 2010

Also, to all those who currently have family members suffering from any form of Dementia.

*To my mother **Eileen McCormack** who died recently, thank you for everything you have ever done for me.*

*My cousin **Mary O'Neill** described you recently as 'a small but mighty woman.' I couldn't agree more.*

'A fly and a flea flew into a flue
Said the fly we must flee
Said the flea we must fly
So they flew through a flaw in the flue'

* * *

'A wonderful bird is the Pelican,
His beak can hold more than his belly
can.
He can keep in his beak,
Enough for a week
And I don't know how the hell he
can!'

Acknowledgements

First and foremost I would like to thank my husband John for his unfailing belief in me, and for his constant love and support no matter what mad scheme I dream up.

My children: Kevin, Carmel, Áine, Aisling, Eileen and Michael are always there for me, so thank you.

Thank you to my brother Dr Seán McCormack, a general practitioner with over 30 years of experience, who cast his medical eye over my story to make sure that I hadn't made any major errors. When we were growing up I just saw him as my baby brother, generally a bit of a nuisance, but really he's worth his weight in gold and generous to a fault.

I would like to thank Nicola Kearns, of *leitrimwritingcottage.com* renowned author and mentor who encouraged and directed me in my dream of becoming a writer. She also makes the most delicious homemade soup!

Noelle Marks of Shanroe Photography, thanks for being such great fun while working your magic to produce my author photo.

To Margaret Finnegan of An Tobar Wellness Centre, thanks for reading the final draft and for your encouraging comments. Margaret's mother Libby is living with Vascular Dementia, so Margaret was the perfect person to review this book.

Many thanks to Steven Weekes for type setting and book layout, and to Finán Callaghan for the cover design, you have made a beautiful book out of my scribbles.

Thank you to my son Michael, who at the age of 10, read the first draft of this story and pronounced it 'deadly'.

Finally I would like to thank my grandchildren for bringing so much extra joy and laughter into my life.

Bernie

TABLE OF CONTENTS

Acknowledgements   *vi*

Prologue   *xiii*

Chapter 1
GRANDAD GETS LOST   I

Chapter 2
A NEW FRIEND   4

Chapter 3
GRANDAD IN THE NIP!   IO

Chapter 4
A FLY AND A FLEA   I3

Chapter 5
MICHAEL'S BIRTHDAY   I9

Chapter 6
WHEN THE PARTY WAS OVER...   25

Chapter 7
A DAY AT JACK'S HOUSE   30

Chapter 8
A NASTY SHOCK   34

Chapter 9
A LUCKY ESCAPE   38

Chapter 10
DAFFODIL LODGE   43

Chapter 11
THE FOOTBALL FINAL   51

Chapter 12
PRESENTATION EVENING AT ST. MALACHY'S   60

Epilogue   67

Author's Note   72

PROLOGUE

'My grandad has Alz-eye-murs!' six year old Michael said proudly, bobbing his head vigorously up and down, so that the vivid orange curls on top of his head scattered all round his face.

'He's got *alz-whats-ers*?' asked Conor incredulously, puckering up his nose, just to show that he didn't believe a word of it.

'Alzeyemurs, silly!' Michael paused dramatically for effect. 'It's a DISEEEEEASE!'

'Is it a rash? Like chicken-pox?' Rose asked hopefully, as she picked at the last remaining scab between her eyebrows.

'No,' said Michael slowly. 'At least I don't *think* so.'

'A rash, just an old mouldy rash,' said Conor scornfully. 'My grandad had a *real* heart attack!'

Michael was saved from answering, when Miss

Treanor turned and glared at them. 'Michael Mulligan, I suppose you have your picture done?' she said sarcastically, in her sugary sweet voice. 'If you are not finished when the bell rings, you will stay in at break time to do it!'

Rose and Conor sniggered as Michael sulkily opened his book.

Two years later...

In the most cheerful voice he could manage, Michael looked directly into Grandad's face and said loudly, 'Hallo Grandad!'

'Oh, hallo Brock,' said Grandad beaming. 'Where have you been?'

'I've been at school - yuck,' said Michael, grinning at Grandad and laughing at his nickname.

'Run and get Grandad a cup of milk please Michael,' said Mum as she tried and failed to put a rug over grandad's knees. It was cold and dry today, and he was sitting on the garden seat. As soon as she had the blanket tucked around her father's legs he kicked it off again.

'Do you have to make more work for me all the time?' she exclaimed as she bent down to pick it up, and was immediately sorry for her harsh words.

'You know I'm just tired,' she said in an undertone, as Michael arrived with a small plastic tumbler full of warm milk.

'Oh, Hallo Brock,' said Grandad beaming. 'Where have you been?'

'School,' said Michael, shortly.

'No need to be cross young man,' Grandad said. 'I only asked you a question! Now in *my* young days, when an adult asked you a question you had *manners.*'

Grandad looked down at his slightly twisted fingers, with the swollen knuckles, and turned them this way and that as if examining them for *manners.* Glancing up again, he suddenly caught Michael's eye.

'Oh, hallo Brock,' he said beaming. 'Where have you been?'

Another year later…

Chapter 1

GRANDAD GETS LOST

It was the whispered voices that attracted Michael's attention; the low urgent rumble of adult worries replaced the usual sound of *Who Wants to be a Millionaire?* on the TV. Wishing he had an extendible ear like his hero *Harry Potter*, Michael crept downstairs, remembering to avoid the squeaky seventh step, and crouched with his ear to the door straining to make out the words. His heart thumped heavily in his chest when he realised his Mum was crying.

'I told him to stay in the car,' she sobbed over and over again.

'Of course you did Joan,' said Daddy. 'How could you have known he was going to get out of the car? It's not as if he has gone anywhere on his own in the last six months.'

'I was only about ten minutes in the butchers, and when I came back I saw the car door wide open …

and no sign of him. Thomas had spotted him and brought him into the café for a cup of tea. He told Thomas that he was going to school.'

'*School*?' said Daddy, trying not to laugh. 'Isn't he a bit long in the tooth for school! How did you find him?'

Mum was beginning to see the funny side of it.

'I ran up and down the street and Thomas saw me. When I went in, there he was, telling everyone he had lost his schoolbag!'

As someone started to move around the kitchen, Michael sprang up and dashed up the stairs, completely forgetting about the seventh step. With a telltale groan the step creaked and two seconds later the kitchen door opened.

'Are you asleep Michael?' asked a stern voice.

'Honestly, PARENTS!' thought Michael. 'If I say yes, then I'm *obviously* not asleep, and if I say no, then Daddy is going to come up to check on me.'

He settled for a sort of sleepy grunt, hoping that Daddy's voice wasn't going to wake Grandad again.

'Keep your voice down, Liam,' Mum said. 'I just couldn't stick it if my Dad decides to sing all night again tonight!'

Michael couldn't agree more. Mum had yelled, 'Michael! Go to bed!' and then Grandad must have sung, *Are you right there Michael, are you right?* one hundred, thousand, MILLION times last night.

He grinned to himself under the duvet, as he pictured his grandad on The X Factor:

Simon Cowell would say 'What are you going to sing for us today, Mr Manning?'

Grandad would pause and answer in his swankiest voice:

'I forget!'

Chapter 2

A NEW FRIEND

Silverstones is a small rural town, 25 miles from Navan in County Meath. On the main street it boasts a post office, a pub, a butcher's shop, a hairdressers, a café and a smattering of houses. The Navan road runs into Main Street, and is mainly a residential area, with neat houses lining each side of the road. Michael lives in one of these houses, the yellow one, in the centre of a terrace of ten houses.

Each house is a modest two-storey, with a small front garden, every garden separated from the next, by railings, or fences, or small low walls. The back gardens are long and narrow, running parallel to each other.

Michael loves his back garden, because unlike most of the gardens, his is just a strip of grass, where he can play football all day long. Mum spends all her time minding Grandad, and doesn't have time to garden. His Daddy is a lorry driver and is away from home quite a lot.

Running at right angles to Main Street is Ballybeeny Road. Taking up one corner of the junction, there is a grocery store with a large car park behind it. St. Malachy's Primary School is next door to the supermarket car park. It is a large school, as three rural schools have closed and this school serves the whole of Drumnaboy Parish. Directly opposite the supermarket, sitting astride the other corner, is the bank.

The school playing field is behind the bank, on the opposite side of the road to the school, and is the pride and joy of Silverstones. Just past the end of the football pitch, there is a brand new 35-bed nursing home, Daffodil Lodge.

If you travel on down Ballybeeny Road, past the school playing field, you will come to St Malachy's Chapel, surrounded by the crumbling stones and crypts of the old graveyard. The *new* graveyard can be seen in the distance, stretching over the hill behind the chapel, the smart new gravestones standing bleakly on the horizon.

***

'Hi Michael,' said Rose, next morning. 'Did your grandad get home all right? My Dad said he was wandering around town yesterday.' Rose's parents owned the café.

'Oi, Ginger!' yelled Conor, as soon as he saw Michael, putting on a gooey ga ga baby voice, to roars of laughter from everyone he stammered:

'Did ... did ... did little lost grandad come home? Did he? Did he?'

'Shut up Conor!' said Michael, clenching his fists, his face turning as red as his hair.

'My Mum says your Grandad is *barmy*,' persisted Conor, tapping his forehead significantly and glancing around at his supporters to see who was listening. 'I heard her saying that Jim Manning wasn't right in the head!'

'Go away and leave me alone!' fumed Michael. 'You're supposed to be my *friend*!'

'Hah! Who'd want to be friends with a loser?' said Conor, his short black hair vivid against his white mean face. He was a tall boy for his age, and while Michael wasn't exactly *small*, he didn't want to fight.

To jeers and roars of laughter, Michael stumbled into the classroom swallowing hard. The rest of the morning was a nightmare as Michael tried to ignore the whispers that seemed to follow him everywhere … batty, loony, nutcase.

***

'Come on' said Rose, at lunchtime. 'I'm going to the library. Do you want to come?'

Michael looked at the sun streaming through the narrow slit, between the blind and the edge of the window. He always played football on good days, Rose knew that, but he really, *really* couldn't face the gang today.

'OK,' he said unhappily, and as an afterthought in a small voice added, 'Thanks.'

'Right, come on then Misery Guts,' said Rose, with her infectious grin.

'Race you!'

'Rose Duffy and Michael Mulligan?' Miss Treanor's acid voice stopped them in their tracks.

'Extra homework for running in the corridor!'

Oh no, thought Michael. This day is just going from bad to worse.

***

Pushing open the door to the library, Michael and Rose were surprised to see Jack there before them.

'Hi,' said Rose.

Jack looked at them, blinked, and answered quietly, 'Oh, … hi.'

Jack was the quietest boy in the class, in the whole *school*, in the whole *world*, Michael thought. In fact, most of the time you just forgot he was there at all. Of course the teachers just *loved* him! The gang had given up annoying him, as he just didn't answer them at all. Michael flushed with embarrassment as he thought of the number of times they had all shouted, 'Noisy Jack,' at him.

'Just don't answer them at all, Michael,' he said in his thoughtful voice, without once looking up from his book.

Michael was so shocked that Jack had spoken at *all*, that he promptly fell across a schoolbag on the floor.

As he sat stunned on the floor, a deep giggle erupted from the corner of Jack's mouth, and Michael found himself smiling back.

Maybe today wasn't such a bad day after all!

Chapter 3

GRANDAD IN THE NIP!

'Do you want to bring your new friend over to play on Saturday?' asked Mum, a couple of weeks later.

'No way!' shouted Michael, in a panic.

How could he *possibly* bring *anyone* to play at his house? You never knew *what* Grandad was going to do next. What if he did the same as yesterday? YIKES! Michael went hot and cold at the very thought of it.

Grandad had come out of his bedroom and walked into the kitchen *with no clothes on*! Not a stitch on him. Stark naked! (Except for his socks!) In spite of himself, Michael began to grin at the memory. Boy, was Mum mad at Grandad.

Even worse, just as Mum was getting Grandad back to his room, there was a knock at the door. Peeping out the window, Michael saw that it was Carol Macken, Conor's mother.

'For God's sake, keep her at the door for five minutes,' hissed Mum, 'Till I get Grandad dressed.'

Michael took his time to open the door and phew, the coast was clear.

'Where's your Mum?' she asked, in her high-pitched, whiny voice.

'She'll be with you in just a minute,' Michael answered, reluctantly.

'Is that grandfather of yours annoying everyone again?' she persisted.

'No, he's not!' Michael lied. 'He's brilliant. He's just fantastic, he's …'

'Yes, *sure*,' said Mrs Macken. 'Well, tell your Mum I called to see did she want a hand. Why on earth she won't put him into the home, I can't understand.'

'*This* is his home,' said Michael fiercely, trying, and failing, to stop angry tears of frustration from spilling down his cheeks.

'Would you look at you, nine years of age and

crying over that grandad of yours, sure he's *not all there* son.'

'I'm not nine. I'm *nearly* ten!' Michael had shouted indignantly, as if that made any difference.

'Cry-ba, cry-ba, look at the ginger cry-ba,' Conor, and his buddies Josh and Keith had sniggered at school today, but Michael was learning a lot from Jack, and pretended he couldn't hear them.

'You know Jack mightn't pass any remarks on your Grandad,' said Mum, breaking into Michael's thoughts about the day before. 'Rose doesn't mind him!'

'Yes, but that's different, Rose knows what he's like Mum,' protested Michael.

There was just *no chance* that Michael was bringing Jack home.

Chapter 4

A Fly and a Flea

'I can't understand it,' said Michael, a few days later. 'How can Grandad remember the silliest things, when he can't remember how to butter his bread?'

Michael, Rose and their silent shadow Jack, were sitting in the canteen while the sun was streaming in the window, making Michael feel very cross and sweaty. He *still* hadn't gone back to playing football at lunchtime and it was making him feel very frustrated, despite Rose annoying him all the time to go back to it.

'Yesterday evening,' continued Michael, 'there was a fly buzzing around the kitchen and Grandad started to go, buzz, buzz, buzz, buzzzzzz.'

Rose and Jack dissolved into giggles as Michael continued.

'And then *all* night he kept rhyming over and over again …'

Michael put on an adult voice and at top speed said:

'A fly and a flea flew into a flue
Said the fly we must flee
Said the flea we must fly
So they flew through a flaw in the flue'

'And he got it right every time! I couldn't believe it. The funniest part is that he hadn't talked to any of us at all for the last few days – a bit like you Jack!' grinned Michael, digging Jack in the ribs with his elbow.

Jack smiled and nodded.

'Why *don't* you talk to us?' puzzled Rose. 'It's not as if you *can't* talk.'

Jack just shrugged his shoulders. He was a tall lanky child for his age, with large hands and long narrow fingers. A very clever boy, when he did speak it was usually only to answer a teacher's question, with one word if possible. Most of the teachers had given up asking him questions at all, because they didn't want to wait for a one-word answer. His school and homework were *always* done perfectly.

'I know,' said Rose. 'Your brain is so busy working everything out all the time, that you don't get round to talking!'

'Ha ha,' laughed Michael. 'Well, you make up for Rosie-Posie don't you Jack? I mean do you ever *stop* talking, Rose?'

'Very funny, *not*,' said Rose, pretending to be offended.

'Michael, go play football,' said Jack suddenly, his deep voice startling both Rose and Michael.

'OK Noisy!' laughed Michael, and he went to his bag, took out his football boots and cheerfully started to lace them up, as Rose looked on astounded.

'How come you wouldn't go when I told you to?' she asked peevishly. 'And how come you talked there now?' she rounded on Jack, crossly.

'Just,' said Jack simply. 'You two are my friends.'

***

'How was football?' asked Rose, after lunchtime.

'Not too bad I suppose,' Michael whispered back, keeping an eye on Miss Treanor. He really didn't want to get extra homework today. As the afternoon wore on, Michael thought about the game.

'So the cry baby is back,' Conor had sneered, as soon as Michael ran out onto the pitch.

'Shut up, Conor,' said Ben. 'We want Ginger on the school team.'

And that was that.

***

Michael's heart sank as he pushed open the gate. He could hear Grandad shouting from here.

'What are you looking at? Are you looking for a fight or what?' said Grandad, propelling himself suddenly out of his chair, taking everyone by surprise as he stood on two very wobbly legs, squaring up to Doctor Maguire.

'There now Mr Manning, calm down please,' said

the doctor. "I'm trying to give you your medicine.'

'Oh no you're not. *I* know what you're doing. You're trying to *poison* me. You want my money...'

'Grandad, if you don't stop, I'll poison you myself,' said Joan. 'Now sit down again before you fall.' As Grandad's legs went from under him, Joan and the doctor got him back into his chair.

'I'm just going to take your blood pressure, Jim,' said Dr Maguire quietly, but with one swipe from Grandad, the monitor landed on the other side of the room.

'Hallo, Grandad,' said Michael, putting his two hands on Grandad's knees, his young face exactly at the same level as the old man. 'Are you being bold again?'

'Hallo Brock,' said Grandad, and, pointing a shaking finger at mum and the doctor, he whispered loudly. 'Do you see those two over there? Who are they? They're trying to poison me. They want my money!'

'Ha, ha, Grandad. Very funny. You don't *have* any money. That's my Mum and the doctor. Come on, behave yourself and take your medicine. I'll do my homework and then we'll watch the match on telly.'

'OK. Whatever you say,' said Grandad meekly.

***

Michael strained to make out the voices in the hallway, but he could only hear parts of the conversation:

'... not safe to stay at home ... needs residential care ... Daffodil Lodge ... hurt someone'

And Mum's indignant voice, slightly raised, carried easily into the sitting room. No way! He wouldn't hurt a *fly*!'

'Fly? What fly?' said Grandad. 'A fly and a flea flew into a flue ...'

Fifteen minutes and fifteen *thousand* flies later, Michael was definitely ready to swat his Grandad.

Chapter 5

MICHAEL'S BIRTHDAY

The morning of Michael's tenth birthday arrived bright and sunny, and normally this would have put him in great form, whooping with delight at his birthday *and* sunshine, but *this* morning he was feeling cross. He was as cranky as his grandad, Mum said.

And it was all because his parents said he had to invite Conor to his birthday party that evening.

'They are our neighbours,' said Mum, as if *that* explained everything.

'That doesn't mean we have to be friends!' Michael had shouted at Mum, but of course parents never listen to you, and Daddy had said,

'Conor is coming and that's that, or you don't get your tickets to the football final.'

'Morning Brock,' said Grandad. 'Why are you like a briar this morning?'

Michael sighed. Grandad seemed to be the only one making sense today.

***

Later that night as he lay in bed, Michael thought about what a strange day it had been. To start with the party had been much better than he had imagined it would be. There was just Rose, Jack, Ben, Conor and Rose's friend Emily, a tall pretty girl, who had just moved to the area from County Tyrone, and who was *deadly* at football. Of course Conor didn't *dare* to be nasty when none of his own friends were there.

They spent a fantastic hour playing football, where Daddy had erected a set of goal posts in the garden for his birthday, while Rose and Jack played a very long game of chess. Which of course Jack won.

In fact, everything had been going fine, the sausages and chips were yummy and Michael had just blown out the candles on his cake, when the trouble began.

Grandad had been sitting quietly in his big chair near the window when he started to mumble and grumble under his breath. Michael felt slightly panicky, but Mum and Dad had *promised* that Grandad would behave.

'Get him out, get him out, what's he doing here?' Grandad roared so suddenly that Emily spilled her coke all over the table, and Michael nearly choked on his cake.

'Go away. Go on … scram!' yelled Grandad, as Daddy tried to pacify him, while Mum and Emily cleaned up the mess.

Grandad was beside himself. 'Put him out, I tell you!'

'Who Grandad?' asked Michael, watching Conor smirking to himself.

'The dog!' said Grandad, as everyone looked around in astonishment.

'What dog?' asked Rose, bewilderedly.

'That one!' said Grandad, and he dived out of his chair so suddenly, that he would certainly have fallen if Daddy hadn't caught him and plonked him back down again.

'There's no dog here,' explained Mum, calmly.

'Of course there is Joan. Do you think I'm stupid or what?' asked Grandad. 'There he is. There. Under the table.'

Eight heads immediately looked under the table, where all they saw was each other's surprised faces hanging upside down.

'He's over at the telly now,' said Grandad, matter of factly.

Everyone looked towards the television. For the next five minutes, there was the strangest game of hide and seek ever. Grandad, getting crosser and crosser, yelled out where the dog was now. The children giggling pretending to look for it, the adults scratching their heads, and everyone telling Grandad there *was* no dog.

Everyone except Jack of course, who hadn't spoken at all, except to say thanks to Mum for the slice of birthday cake.

When Jack suddenly spoke, everyone was startled, even Grandad.

'Mr. Manning, I'll put the dog out,' he said, and

going over to the door he calmly opened it.

'Come on boy,' he said, making clucking noises with his tongue. 'Good boy. Out you go! Go on. Shoo!'

And then he closed the door.

And there was silence in the kitchen.

'Thanks,' said Mum gratefully, when she recovered from the surprise.

***

'Could you *really* see a dog?' demanded Rose, when they had all gone back out to the garden. 'And you *have* to answer me Jack,' she said fiercely, 'Or I will never never, never, never, *never* speak to you again!'

'OK, he gets the picture,' said Ben grinning. 'I want to know too!'

'No, *I* couldn't see a dog, but Mr. Manning could!' said Jack. 'So I thought I better get rid of it.'

'Go to the bathroom now children, before you go home,' said Mum, as his friends were leaving, as if they were all *two* years of age and not *ten*.

'What's he up to?' thought Michael suspiciously, as Conor came back from the bathroom, with a strange glint in his eye, as if he had just discovered something *very, very,* interesting.

Chapter 6

WHEN THE PARTY WAS OVER...

The following morning, as soon as Michael walked into the schoolyard, he saw the group of children huddled around Conor.

'I'm telling you, he shouts, he dribbles, he sees ghost dogs, and you'll never guess what else,' Conor was playing his audience well, waiting to make sure he had everyone's attention. 'He wears *giant nappies!*'

'Adults don't wear nappies,' said Ben, when the howls of laughter had died down.

'Well, Ginger's grandad does,' retorted Conor. 'Did you not see the stack of *enormous* nappies on the shelf in the bathroom?'

Michael stood frozen to the spot. Too late he remembered that he hadn't put the pile of nappies into the cupboard when his Mum had told him to. The children began to nudge each other and snigger as someone spotted Michael.

'There he is!' shouted Keith, one of Conor's followers, pointing a derisory finger in his direction. 'Ha, look at him. Just standing there as if he didn't have a nutty grandad who wears *nappies*!'

'Nappies, nappies, nappies!'

The chant rang in Michael's ears, as tears stung his eyes.

'He's crying now. He's a big baby. Just like his grandad!' jeered Conor.

'I'm *not* crying,' yelled Michael. 'My eyes are leaking!'

He turned and ran blindly towards the school gate almost knocking over Jack, Rose and Emily who stood blocking his way.

'You can't run away from it, you know,' said Jack quietly. 'Do you want to come to my house on Saturday? My big brother is nineteen. He has Down's Syndrome and he sometimes wears nappies.'

Michael stood still in shock. So *that's* why Jack never talked about his family.

'But everyone knows about Down's Syndrome, so what difference does that make to *you*?' said Michael accusingly.

'You'd be surprised how many people laugh and point at you whenever they meet Gary,' said Jack.

'Most people pass no remarks. It's only the silly ones who laugh!' said Emily. 'Come on Michael, you *can't* go home, we need you for the football at lunchtime.'

Rose was standing still, staring at Jack …

'You are the most *annoying* boy *ever*,' she fumed. 'You don't talk to us at all, and then you suddenly tell us all this. Did you not trust us enough to tell us?'

'Sorry,' said Jack, a little ashamed of himself now. 'I just don't like talking about it. And I didn't like my last school.'

'That's OK,' said Rose, her sunny nature returning. 'Come on, or we'll all be late and Miss Treanor will make us stay in at break time.'

***

'Who are you? What are you doing in my house?' asked a quivering voice, when Michael walked through the door that evening.

'It's *me* Grandad. Brock,' said Michael as his heart sank to his boots.

School had been OK, because his friends had stood up for him, and he had just ignored Conor and his gang. But now for the first time Grandad didn't know him.

'Brock? What a daft name! When *I* was a boy, children had proper names, like John, or Thomas, or James ... who *are* you?'

'I'm Michael. You're my Grandad and you're the only one who calls me Brock!' grinned Michael, suddenly seeing the funny side of it. The name Brock was a special secret between him and his grandad.

'Do you know why you call me Brock, Grandad?' asked Michael, smiling.

Grandad was puzzled.

'No ... why?' he asked.

'When I was little,' explained Michael, 'with my big head of orange curls, you said I looked like a lump of ginger broccoli, so you called me Brock for short! We never told Mum … she would probably yell, I suppose.'

Grandad laughed and laughed. Then he stopped. He looked at Michael.

'Oh, hallo Brock,' he said, beaming. 'Where have you been?'

And the familiar routine began again.

Chapter 7

A Day At Jack's House

S aturday morning dawned cold and bright. Jack lived in the countryside four miles the other side of town, so Mum had to drive him there. Michael was feeling a little bit scared of meeting Jack's family, especially Gary, but Mum assured him that he would have great fun.

As the car pulled up outside the gate, Jack came round the side of the house followed by a very big fellow, with the biggest smile Michael had ever seen.

'Hallo Michael, are you Jack's friend?' asked Gary, engulfing Michael's hand with his two hands, and giving him a vigorous handshake. 'Welcome to our house.'

'Thanks!' said Michael, when he had got his hand and arm back.

The whole day passed in a flurry of fun. First they played the Play Station, and then they played Hide and Seek, which was hilarious because Gary was much too big to fit anywhere.

'I can see you, Gary!' laughed Michael, as he spotted two broad shoulders and two large feet sticking out either side of the trunk of a narrow ash tree.

'Ah no! You found me *again*,' moaned Gary.

Jack was just as quiet at home as he was at school, just speaking the odd time, spending his time happily listening to Gary chattering.

'Your brother is *cool*.' said Michael. 'I wish *I* had a brother!'

'I only see Gary at the weekends. He goes to a special school in Dublin,' Jack said suddenly.

'Oh, right. You must miss him a lot,' said Michael, as Jack nodded his head.

'Football. Football!' shouted Gary, as he came out of his room carrying an ancient leather O'Neill's ball. The boys dashed outside, where Jack positioned himself calmly between the two ash trees. He flexed his large hands with the long narrow fingers and grinned at Michael and Gary.

'Not *fair*!' yelled Gary, as Jack saved yet another shot, blasted at him from 10 metres out.

'Yes, fair,' smiled Jack, as he pulled off yet another spectacular save.

An hour and a half later, the two younger boys were exhausted, while Gary *still* seemed to have endless energy.

'I give up,' said Michael to Gary. 'You win!'

'Ha, I always win!' said Gary happily, as Jack nodded cheerfully.

***

It was a very tired Michael who arrived home at his own house later that evening.

'I had a *fantastic* day,' he told his grandad. 'Gary is *brilliant* at football.'

'Football?' said Grandad. 'Do I like football?'

'Of course you do Grandad! Sure you played for the County years ago. Will I get your box of medals so we can look at them again?'

'OK,' said Grandad vaguely, as Michael sped off to get the old biscuit tin where they were stored.

They spent a happy half hour examining the medals. Michael didn't mind that his grandad didn't remember any of it; he knew the stories off by heart. When he was little he was *always* pestering Grandad to tell his epic tales of games won and lost.

Michael got a tissue and gently wiped Grandad's nose. This is very strange, he thought, as he washed his hands,

'I'm telling Grandad the stories of when *he* was young, and not the other way around. Everything *really* is backwards!'

Chapter 8

A NASTY SHOCK

❛ It's time to consider other options, Mrs Mulligan,' said Dr. Maguire, as he was examining Grandad's chest with the stethoscope. Grandad didn't even blink. He had been like that for the last few weeks.

Jim Manning had sunk into a world where he didn't know any of them, was very cross, wouldn't eat anything *and* was finding it difficult to breathe.

Yet *sometimes*, Grandad seemed to waken up, and was in great form, watching football and spouting poetry.

'You know Daffodil Lodge have rooms available at the moment,' continued the doctor, 'And all the nurses and carers are fully trained. I call there twice a week to examine the patients. I'm beginning to worry about your *own* health, Joan.'

But Michael's mum was stubborn.

'As long as I'm able to, I want to keep him at home,' she insisted.

'Well, at least think about it,' said Dr. Maguire. 'You know that you want him to be as comfortable as possible, at the end.'

Michael ran up the stairs to his room, and buried his face in his pillow so that no one would hear his sobs.

He *knew* he shouldn't have been listening at the door. He didn't want to think about what, 'THE END,' meant. And he didn't want to think about the smart new gravestones, straddling the hill in the distance.

Michael woke up to someone gently shaking his shoulder.

'Michael, I know you heard what Dr. Maguire said, you forgot the creaky step again!' said Mum.

In spite of himself Michael smiled.

'We all just want the best for your Grandad, and if Daffodil Lodge seems the best idea we'll have to go with it,' said Mum, with tears in her eyes.

'Now come on, I have to take Grandad into hospital for some tests, so I'm dropping you off at Jack's house.'

***

Even in the short journey to Jack's house, Grandad had been awkward, thought Michael that night. After they had got him into the car, a *mammoth* task on its own, he had been insisting that he didn't know who they were.

'Why are you tying me up?' he had wailed piteously.

(That was the seatbelt of course!)

'I'm going to jump out!' he'd howled.

'For God's sake, put the child lock on the door Michael,' said Mum, as Grandad was making his *third* attempt to escape.

Afterwards, Michael wondered how come he didn't realise something was wrong. Both himself and Jack had *heard* the wailing sirens of the fire brigade and the ambulance.

They were playing the Play Station, and had rushed to the window to see both vehicles screaming past the house.

And then they went on with their games.

It was later, much later in the evening, that Jack's Mum had called the two boys in and said, 'Michael you're staying the night with us, is that OK?'

'Yeeess!' said Michael.

Suddenly, he noticed Marie's face.

Icy fingers of fear clutched his stomach.

Just at that moment, Brian, Jack's father arrived home from work.

'Hi Marie,' he said, giving his wife a kiss, not noticing the two boys.

'Did you hear there's been an accident down on Ballybeeney road? A van and a small red car?'

Brian stopped talking, as too late, he realised that his wife was frantically shaking her head at him, and that there were two small, white, terrified faces staring at him in absolute horror.

Chapter 9

A LUCKY ESCAPE

Afterwards, everyone said that it was lucky that no one was killed, and that only for Conor and his Mum, both Joan *and* Grandad could have been dead.

Carol had been driving behind Mum at the time, and had seen it all happening. She had called the emergency services immediately.

The van driver was in a state of shock, his eyes glazed, his hands glued to the steering wheel.

Carol and Conor had scrambled across the ditch and down the bank to the battered car. They managed to break the car windows and wrench open the doors. After Carol had checked their injuries, she undid both seatbelts, and gently turned both of them the right way round, before the ambulance arrived.

'If they had been hanging upside down for one *minute* more, even one *second* more, they would be dead now,' Conor was telling everyone at school.

'Of course, *my* mum is trained in First Aid and *she* knew what to do! But she couldn't have done it without *me*!' he said proudly.

For once, Michael didn't mind Conor going on about it, because he knew it was true. If they hadn't acted so quickly, it could have been very different. Michael didn't really care as long as they were both OK. What were a few broken ribs after all? Even Mum's broken shoulder would fix in time.

He had even managed to mumble, 'Thanks,' to Conor.

The funny part was that he was *sort* of friends with Conor again. Not *best* friends of course, Jack and Rose were his best friends, but at least he wasn't dreading going to school any more.

In fact Conor was telling everyone, as if *he* was an expert,
'Michael's grandad has that disease, *Alzheimer's*, so he *really* doesn't know what he's doing at all. He can't *help* it, you know!'

That week at school, the class was set a project to look up the disease Alzheimer's and to write two pages about it. Michael stared at the computer screen as himself and Jack sat in the library doing their homework:

Alzheimer's disease (AD) is an irreversible, progressive brain disease that slowly destroys memory and thinking skills, and eventually even the ability to carry out the simplest tasks. Symptoms include memory loss, language problems, and unpredictable behaviour. As the disease progresses personality changes may occur and the patient may experience hallucinations.

'Jack … what are hallucinations?'

'I *think* it means that you can see something that's not really there,' answered Jack. 'Why?'

'Read this!' said Michael, and he shoved over on the seat to let Jack see.

'Well, *that* explains the invisible dog,' laughed Jack.

That was another amazing thing, thought Michael to himself. After the night that he had stayed in Jack's house, when he didn't know if Mum and his grandad were going to be OK, Jack had begun to speak a little bit more. Now, although he *still* didn't say much, he would at least talk to Michael, Rose, Emily and Ben.

'Hey, look at this bit,' said Michael, starting to giggle.

> … the brain develops abnormal clumps called amyloid plaques, and tangled bundles of fibres called neurofibrillary tangles …

'I wonder does that mean your brain is like a bowl of spaghetti?'

Both boys dissolved into a fit of laughing, and Mrs McMahon chased them out of the library for disturbing the other pupils.

'Wait till you hear Mum describing the accident,' said Michael to Jack. 'That'll make you laugh even more!'

Joan was quite funny talking about the crash, now that everyone was on the mend.

Having just dropped Michael to Jack's house, she

continued on the road to Navan, driving carefully as this was a notorious stretch of the road, nicknamed locally as the Four Sisters Bends.

On the last of the four corners, Grandad had suddenly yelled, and lunged for the steering wheel, putting Joan directly into the path of an oncoming van.

In the panic to avoid the van, she had careered out of control, straight through the ditch, down a drop of three metres and tumbled over twice, before the Opel Astra came to rest on its roof in the middle of a field of cows.

As the car was tumbling, and pens, keys, an umbrella, a bag of crisps, and a bottle of water rained around her, Joan had the bizarre thought, that she *really* should tidy the car more often!

In the eerie silence that followed, Mum opened her eyes and looked into the upside down face of a curious cow.

Just as she slipped unconscious, out of the gloom she heard Grandad's voice,

'*That was fun*! Can we do it again?'

Chapter 10

DAFFODIL LODGE

Michael slowly walked up the leafy driveway to Daffodil Lodge, kicking a stone ahead of him, paused, changed the angle of his shot ... 'Goal!' he said to himself, as the stone flew neatly between the trunks of the two horse chestnut trees.

He looked up longingly at the branches high over his head. The five-fingered leaves seemed to wave at him, but the chestnuts were still green. He would definitely have the best collection of chestnuts in the class, when autumn came.

Then he scowled, he mightn't have. *Conor* might have the best collection. His mother was now working in Daffodil Lodge. Maybe if we collect them *together*, we might get the best *ever* conkers. He smiled to himself and ran the rest of the way up the drive.

Miraculously, Grandad had only suffered cuts and bruises in the crash, so he had been sent to Daffodil Lodge for respite for a few weeks, while Mum was in hospital.

And he was very happy there.

And he wanted to stay.

The only one who wasn't happy was Mum. It was now four weeks since the accident, and she was still very sore, but the broken ribs and broken shoulder were healing. She was just very sad that Grandad wasn't at home any more.

Michael shook himself, well *he* was very happy. He could visit Grandad any time he wanted, (except for meal times, and who wants to watch other people eating? ... YUK!)

He could bring in his books and read stories to Grandad. He could watch football with him, *and* he could just go home if Grandad was having a bad day.

He couldn't understand why his Mum was crying all the time, but he had overheard Dr Maguire saying to his Daddy that she was suffering from delayed shock and exhaustion.

Grandad was to stay in Daffodil Lodge for 6 months if possible. He hadn't been able to hear the rest, but Daddy told him later that Dr Maguire said Grandad was VERY SICK.

Michael *knew* what that meant. He wished that adults would all stop talking in Capital Letters, and talk to him properly. After all I'm ten now, he thought crossly. I know what they mean by, 'THE END'.

He jabbed the code numbers to open the door to Grandad's unit, plastered a smile on his face, and strolled down the corridor to the sitting room.

***

Michael peeped around the door and scanned the faces. An air of quiet peace pervaded the room today as the residents snoozed or watched afternoon TV.

He saw Sarah, taking up the best chair beside the window as usual. She was a *really* cross old lady, who shouted at everyone whenever she got a chance to. Today she was asleep ... phew!

Kenneth was there in his wheelchair. He had been injured in a rugby match. (He was *forty*, and everyone said he was *young*!)

There was Annie, another old lady, who smiled and said, 'Hello, young man,' every time she saw Michael.

Marian was there too. She was only a little older than his Mum, but had suffered a stroke. Michael found it quite hard to understand her, but he was getting more used to it.

Andrew was parked in the corner in his wheelchair. He was twenty-two, and had been badly injured in a car crash three years ago. He always chatted happily to Michael about football, or school, or the latest films.

But there was no sign of Grandad.

Michael wished that Mum would come in and talk to these people, and see how happy they were. *Then* she would see that they were not *all* really old. There were *lots* of interesting people, besides the nurses and carers, for Grandad to talk to.

'Hallo, Michael,' said a voice behind him, and Michael turned round to smile at Carol. He wasn't afraid of her any more; she seemed to have changed so much since the accident too.

Who would have ever thought that she would be

brilliant with the sick and the old people! She had decided to train as a nurse and was now working part-time as a carer in Daffodil Lodge. The patients liked her no-nonsense approach, and they did *exactly* what she wanted them to.

'Your grandad is up in his room Michael,' she said. 'He's not so good today. He didn't sleep all night, so he's tired and cross'

'OK, thanks Carol,' said Michael, sadly. He had got a wonderful book full of bright pictures of birds and animals to show Grandad, but he could show it to him some other day. *Some* days, when Grandad was in good form, he loved to look at pictures and to chat. He very rarely knew who Michael was now, but he had always liked talking to people.

Grandad was sitting in the big armchair in his room, with a large pillow behind his back, and a blanket covering him, with just the collar of his shirt showing above it. At least he can wear his own clothes, thought Michael. He had imagined that Grandad would be in pyjamas all the time! His head was back and his mouth was open, as he breathed noisily.

Michael grinned. He thought about saying, "BOO!" but Grandad might fall out of the chair with fright, and hurt himself, so he had better not.

He sat down quietly on the little stool, put his own hand over Grandad's big hand and said loudly, 'Hallo, Grandad.'

Grandad struggled to open his eyes, glared at Michael and said, 'Go away!'

'Grandad, it's me, Brock,' said Michael.

'Go away,' said Grandad, louder this time.

'OK, I'll come back later,' said Michael. 'I've a lovely new book to show you.'

But Grandad didn't answer him at all.

***

Michael was worried, Grandad would be seventy-four tomorrow, and he really hoped his Mum would come to visit. What if he was like this tomorrow?

Yesterday he had been sitting up straight in a chair in the sitting room, asking Andrew where the Post Office was, saying he had a letter to post.

Andrew was great fun, thought Michael. After

Grandad had asked about twenty times, he had solemnly taken the folded serviette out of grandad's hand, whizzed out the door in his wheelchair, came back a few seconds later and cheerfully announced:

'There you are, Mr. Manning. I posted it for you!'

A voice broke into his thoughts, as Carol said to him,

'Now Michael, I'm bringing Joan to see your grandad tomorrow. If she won't come with me, I'll sit outside your house and beep the horn until she does!'

Michael burst out laughing. He just *knew* that it would work.

Nobody *dared* to disobey Carol. Everyone else was being n-i-c-e to Mum all the time, and that wasn't working.

When Michael came home from school the next day, he nervously opened the kitchen door.

'Hi, Mum,' he said.

Joan was sitting at the kitchen table, nursing a cup

of coffee with her good hand, her hair had been done, and she smiled at him.

'Hi Michael. How was school today? Why didn't you tell me Daffodil Lodge was such a lovely place? We'll go up again later and bring a birthday cake for Grandad.'

'WHAT????' thought Michael, as a huge weight seemed to lift off his shoulders.

My *real* Mum is back, he thought happily.

Chapter 11

THE FOOTBALL FINAL

It was the day of the primary school's football final, and Michael couldn't swallow his breakfast with excitement. For the first time ever, his school, St Malachy's was into the county final, against St Columban's from Riverdale.

St. Malachy's had won all of their matches over the last couple of weeks, but St. Columban's were last year's champions. Everyone expected St. Columban's to win easily.

'Go out there and give it your best,' said Mr. Rogers, the headmaster. 'And you never know, we might surprise St. Columbans. Play your hearts out, and play fair.'

When they got to the pitch, the full class were told to get togged out, in case there were injuries.

'Huh,' moaned Rose. 'As if *I* want to play football. I'm the cheerleader!' and she danced about grinning and waving her arms wildly around her head.

'If you do that, Rose, the other team will fall down and faint,' answered Michael, with a laugh.

'Hey, maybe that's a good idea!' said Jack, ducking as Rose aimed a swipe at him.

'Ha, ha. Very funny ... not!' she said. 'Come on Jack. Let's get a good spot on the sidelines. Good luck, Emily. Good luck, Michael. Ben, don't let in any goals!'

'Not if I can help it,' answered Ben, glumly. He was feeling very nervous, but he was a brilliant goalie, and the team knew they could rely on him.

The match was being played on the large pitch outside Navan; so that neither of the schools had home advantage. But the entire population of Silverstones seemed to have turned out to support St. Malachy's.

The buses were parked along the side of the road, beside the wire fencing, and suddenly Michael's heart jumped. *There* it was, the white mobility van with the daffodil motif on the side. Brilliant! Carol had organised that a few of the patients, and their carers and family, could come to the final.

There was a special area where people in wheelchairs

could watch matches, so Andrew, Grandad, and anyone else who wanted to, would be in there. Michael waved as he spotted Mum pushing Grandad's wheelchair.

The whistle blew. The ball was thrown up and the game started with a flurry of activity. Emily, their star full forward was a big surprise to the other team. She had height and agility, and between herself and Conor, who had speed and accuracy, St Columban's were taken by surprise. St Malachy's were first on the scoreboard with a fine point from Conor. Then another two points were added. Then Emily scored a goal. St Malachy's supporters were going wild with delight.

But St. Columban's were the champions, and it was easy to see why. They overcame their initial surprise and the scores started to creep up. Michael was in left corner back, marking a tall boy with long wavy hair that flapped up and down when he ran, so that he looked like someone from a shampoo ad. *And* he ran like the wind.

'Come *on*, Ginger!'

Michael could hear his friends shouting, and it spurred him on, to stick like glue to his opponent, and prevent him from scoring. Ben was having a brilliant match. Time and time again, he caught the ball safely, and held it tightly to his chest. Once, he just got his fingers to it and knocked it over the bar for a point, instead of conceding a goal.

The half time score was St. Malachy's one goal and six points to St. Columban's nine points. So the teams were level.

'Right lads!' urged Mr Rogers '... and girls,' he hastily added, as he caught Emily's frown.

They were in the half time huddle, getting advice from their headmaster.

'The pride of the Royal County is at stake here! Do we want to be Meath County Champions or not?' he yelled.

'Yes, *Sir*!' everyone shouted.

'Do we want to win?'

'Yes, *Sir*!'

'Are we going to do our best?'

'Yes, *Sir*!'

'Are we going to be proud of ourselves even if we *don't* win?'

The 'Yes, *Sir*!' was deafening this time.

'OK, St Malachy's, let's make it happen!' said Mr Rogers.

The second half started with St Malachy's playing against the wind. St Columban's edged ahead with a two-point lead. Conor scored a point, then Emily brought them level again with a wonderful score from a free kick. St Columban's started to nudge ahead, but yet again, St Malachy's levelled the game.

The halfbacks and the full backs of St Malachy's were playing the game of their lives, blocking St Columban's forwards, as if their lives depended on it. Michael felt as if his lungs would burst as he continually ran and jumped and tried to keep up with Shampoo Head.

Then Martin, one of the St. Malachy's half forwards, put over two brilliant points, and they were ahead. The roars of the Silverstones supporters were thunderous.

Then ... DISASTER!

Ben came out to capture a loose ball, collided with a St Columban's full forward, and fell sideways, going over awkwardly on his ankle. The trainers ran out onto the field, everyone stopped to catch their breath, and Mr Rogers shook his head.

'That ankle is sprained. You'll have to go off Ben.'

'Oh no!" groaned a white faced Ben. 'Who will go in goals?'

The players looked at each other in despair, none of them were any good in goals. There were plenty of subs for other positions on the field, but no one ever wanted to do goals. They had all done it in training, but Ben had never got injured in a match before today.

'Sir, Sir, *Sir,*' said Michael urgently, as inspiration hit him. 'I know who could do it!' he was almost gabbling with excitement, 'Jack!'

'Jack?'

'Yes, Sir. Really, Sir' said Michael with excitement. 'I've seen him at home. Honest. He's our only hope. The rest of us are rubbish in goals, Sir! He's togged out and all!'

Mr. Rogers scratched his head. He had about three seconds to make up his mind.

'Well, I suppose I could give him a go,' he said slowly. 'There's not much else we can do.'

It was a very surprised Jack that found himself out on the pitch standing between the goal posts.

After a shaky start he did well, catching the ball, kicking out accurately, and picking out his own players easily, as if he had always been on the team. There was nothing either he or Michael could do, as Shampoo Head aimed the ball high in the sky between the goalposts to score a couple of points. The teams were level again. Then St Malachy's nosed ahead by one point.

There were two minutes left to go.

The ball drifted down towards Michael and his marker. Both jumped. Shampoo Head caught it and ran towards the goals with Michael in hot pursuit. In desperation Michael lunged at the ball, caught the jersey of the other player, and the whistle blew.

A penalty for St Columban's.

Complete CATASTROPHE.

This would be the last kick of the game. St Malachy's were leading by a point; a goal is worth three points. If St Columban's scored the penalty, they would snatch the victory.

As if in a fog Michael watched what was happening. He could see the fear in Jack's eyes.

The crowd fell silent.

'Pretend it's Gary!' Michael suddenly shouted to his friend. Jack looked at him, and the nervous look was replaced with one of determination.

Shampoo Head took his time. He placed the ball carefully, looked at it, walked back a few paces, and paused.

Jack flexed his large hands with the long narrow fingers.

Shampoo Head ran forward and struck the ball.

It sailed high towards the top right-hand corner of the net. Jack seemed to fly through the air, and pandemonium broke out as the final whistle blew and the ball was safely cradled in Jack's arms.

The entire population of Silverstones swamped the players of St. Malachy's, but Michael wasn't there. After throwing his arms around his friend, he had raced off the pitch towards the wheelchair area.

'Did you see it Grandad? Did you see it?' he was whooping with delight.

'Who won?' said Grandad, waking up. 'Who are you?'

'We won! I'm Brock and you're my Grandad. I'll be getting a gold medal at the presentation evening and I'll put it in the box with *your* medals,' said Michael, giving his Grandad a big hug and a kiss.

He dashed back to his friends to join them in their lap of honour round the field carrying the coveted McKinley Cup.

'Oh ... OK!' said Grandad.

Chapter 12

PRESENTATION EVENING AT ST. MALACHY'S

I t was the end of year Presentation Evening in St Malachy's Primary School. The pupils and their parents were gathered in the Assembly Hall. Mr Rogers was calling out a long list of awards for each class year, and Michael was fidgeting, because they were starting with the youngest classes.

At last it came to Sixth Class.

Michael sat up straight.

Each class had chosen a person to perform an item for the parents, so Rose had been picked in his class. She walked demurely up to the stage and read out a story she had written for their project on Alzheimer's Disease. When she had finished, she went pink with delight as Mr Rogers praised her work, and said wasn't she a great example to all the children in the school.

She walked quietly off the stage and then to

everyone's amusement, she hopped, skipped and ran the whole way down to her seat beside her parents.

Next up was the football team. Michael thought he would burst with pride as they were formally presented (again!) with the McKinley Cup, and they each received their gold medals.

His hand was sweaty; he was holding his medal so tight. He just couldn't *believe* he had won a county medal, and he couldn't *wait* to put it into the box with all of Grandad's medals. His face hurt from smiling so much, as every parent wanted a photo of the team.

Finally they were allowed back to their seats.

Michael let his mind wander a bit. He was looking forward to the party *after* the presentations. He knew there was no chance that he was going to win *'best mathematics student in sixth class'* or the *'best behaved student!'*

He was a bit surprised and disappointed that Jack didn't win *that* one. *It* went to Monica, a small girl, who was sugary sweet to the teachers, but was mean to some of the other children in the yard.

She smirked with self-importance when she was called up to the stage, and accepted her prize while her classmates clapped unenthusiastically.

Girl's Sports Star of the Year went to Emily, and Boys Sports Star of the Year went to Ben, who hobbled up onto the stage with his crutches, to massive applause. No one except Ben himself was surprised when he was named.

'And now,' said Mr Rogers, and he paused, took off his glasses, rubbed his eyes tiredly, and placed them back on the tip of his nose.

'This year we have a number of Special Awards.'

Michael sat up straighter. So did everyone else. 'Special Awards? We haven't had *that* before!' he thought to himself.

Mrs Fitzsimons, the vice principal, carried up two large, brand new, shiny silver cups to the stage, went in behind the curtains, and came back with an *enormous* bouquet of flowers and a cut-glass bowl.

You could have heard a pin dropping in the hall. Everyone was puzzled.

Mr Rogers suddenly took a fit of coughing, and some of the smaller children began to giggle.

'And now,' said Mr Rogers, when he had recovered and order was restored, 'For the final presentations.'

'Three months ago, on the outskirts of the town, there was a car accident.'

Michael felt the hair beginning to prickle on the back of his neck as everyone was squirming in their seats, trying to get a look at him and his parents. His Mum and Daddy were beaming. He suspected they knew what was coming next.

Mr Rogers was continuing:

'That accident could have been fatal, but for the quick actions of one of our young students, and his mother. On behalf of St. Malachy's School, the Mulligan family, and the community of Siverstones, I would like to invite Carol and Conor Macken to the stage to receive their special awards for bravery, and for helping to save lives.'

To thunderous applause, Carol and Conor made their way to the stage. Michael's hands were sore from clapping, and Carol's face was priceless - a mixture of shock, embarrassment and pride as she accepted her glass bowl and the flowers.

Conor was presented with one of the two large shiny cups and was so excited he jumped up and down like a kangaroo!

When the cheers and claps had died down, and everyone had returned to their seats, there was still one cup left on stage.

There was silence in the hall.

'The final presentation this evening, ladies and gentlemen, goes to a student who is excellent at his schoolwork, copes well with all manner of difficulties, and is well respected as a valuable member of our school, by both the teachers and the students themselves.'

The crowd was still … waiting, wondering. No one had any idea who was going to be named.

Mr. Rogers continued; '… He also pulled off the best penalty save I have ever seen in Primary School Championship Football!'

The entire assembly hall was up standing, as a white-faced Jack was clapped on the back and practically shoved up onto the stage to receive the silver cup for an outstanding contribution to St Malachy's Primary School.

When Jack was presented with the award, he said nothing. First, he looked at the floor, and then just lifted his head enough to grin shyly at Mr Rogers, and then at the audience.

What a wonderful finish to a school year that had started off so miserably, thought Michael to himself, as he made his way to the canteen for the party.

Rose chattered happily to Jack, who was smiling and nodding his head. Then Jack said something to Rose, and Michael could see Rose cracking up with laughter. Emily and Ben were very excited, examining their sports awards.

Michael was dawdling behind them, when he realised that Conor was at his elbow. For a moment there was an awkward silence.

'Sorry for being so mean to you earlier in the year!' Conor blurted out suddenly, blushing bright red with embarrassment.

'Ah, that's OK,' Michael said quickly. 'Thanks for saving Mum and Grandad!'

The two boys looked at each other solemnly, and then they started to laugh. They really didn't know what they were laughing at, but it felt good anyway.

'Come on you two,' called Rose. 'Wait till you hear this. Jack is after telling me a *joke*! What do you call a boomerang that doesn't work?'

'What???' asked Michael and Conor together.

'A stick!'

Michael laughed till the tears ran down his face.

Jack telling jokes? What next? he thought to himself.

And Jack just looked around at all his friends, and smiled.

Epilogue

Balancing his precious medal on top of the big picture book that he had forgotten to leave back to the library, Michael pushed open the door to Grandad's room. The door was heavier than he thought, and the medal slid off the shiny plastic book cover and landed with a clunk, tinkle, tinkle onto the ground.

Grandad woke with a start.

Not a good idea to wake Grandad suddenly. Michael froze … and waited. Luckily Grandad didn't shout and roar like he sometimes did if something startled him.

'I can't find my Mammy,' he said plaintively. 'Will you find her for me?'

'Of course I will,' said Michael, 'But first I want to show you my gold medal and my book.'

Grandad was now mostly confined to bed or to his chair, but his speech was still quite clear.

'I'm Brock, you're my Grandad,' said Michael, 'and you used to be a *brilliant* footballer. Look I've got a county medal, just like your ones.'

'Oh!' Now Grandad was interested.

'And just look at the book I've brought you!'

Michael perched on the handle of Grandad's chair and started to show him all the pictures. Grandad's eyes weren't so vacant today. Now and again he asked,

'What's that?'

'That's a crocodile,' answered Michael. 'Wow! Look at his teeth! And look at the tiny birds cleaning them! They're called Plovers. It says here, that the plovers get a free meal and the crocodiles get clean teeth! Ha, ha. That's very funny, isn't it?'

Grandad didn't answer.

Michael turned each page, chatting easily to Grandad about the pictures, sometimes getting a response, sometimes not.

'Guess what Grandad? It says here that elephants are the only animals to have four knees! And do you know how many eyes a bee has? Five! Imagine that!'

'Look at the pelicans,' said Michael, admiring the funny looking birds.

'Hey, listen to this:'

Pelicans and their relatives are strong swimmers and are the only birds with webbing between all four toes.

'Did you know that Grandad?'

'Pelican, pelican, pelican, pelican, pelican,' said Grandad, in a puzzled voice, rolling the word around in his mouth like a toffee.

"Pelican, pelican, pelican, pelican ... pelican? ... pelican?"

A wonderful bird is the Pelican,
His beak can hold more than his belly can.
He can keep in his beak,
Enough for a week
And I don't know how the hell he can!'

Michael laughed till his sides hurt. Trust Grandad to come up with a rhyme about a pelican.

'Pelican, pelican …his beak is a week … no … in his belly… no,' said Grandad, getting confused.

'A wonderful bird is the pelican…'

And off he went again.

And again.

And again.

And again.

And again.

And again.

'Oh no,' thought Michael, ten minutes later, as he kissed his Grandad goodnight, popped his gold medal into his pocket and left the animal book on the bedside locker.

As he went down the corridor, Grandad's voice

floated gently after him,

'Pelican, pelican, pelican, pelican, pelican...'

Michael knew that Grandad didn't know him. He also knew that his grandad wasn't going to get any better. But he loved him, and would keep visiting him as often as he could.

THE END would surely come, maybe soon enough, maybe not.

He would deal with it as best he could, whenever it *did* happen.

For now he was going home to his own house. He wanted to get a good night's sleep. Tomorrow was Saturday, and he had football practise at 10am. After that he was going to Jack's house to play.

He idly kicked a stone, left foot, right foot, dodged an imaginary player,

'Yes!'

He punched the air as the stone flew neatly between the trunks of the horse chestnut trees,

'Goal!'

On the 15th January 2010, at the age of 99, my dad, Dr John McCormack, passed away. He had suffered from Senile Dementia for about 5 years.

During that time, I watched the father I knew and loved, become someone quite different.

It was heart-breaking to watch a man who was my hero, change from being a gentle, loving person, into someone who was at times rude, angry, aggressive or unresponsive.

And yet at other times I caught glimpses of my real dad.

The rhymes 'The Fly and the Flea' and 'The Pelican' were favourites of his, and sometimes he repeated them incessantly, much to the amusement and probable annoyance of everyone around him.

My children were young at the time, and being with their grandad had a profound effect on them.

Dad moved into Blackrock Abbey Nursing Home in Dundalk about 3 years before he died, where he received excellent care.

I wrote this book during the last 6 months of my dad's life and finished it just weeks before he died.

It has taken me until now to pluck up the courage to publish it.

Bernie Muckian

Lightning Source UK Ltd.
Milton Keynes UK
UKHW010709020123
414699UK00009B/304